A Note to Parents and Caregivers:

With a focus on math, science, and social studies, *Read-it!* Readers support both the learning of content information and the extension of more complex reading skills. They encourage the development of problem-solving skills that help children expand their thinking.

 The PURPLE LEVEL presents basic topics and objects using high frequency words and simple language patterns.

 The RED LEVEL presents familiar topics using common words and repeating sentence patterns.

 The BLUE LEVEL presents new ideas using a larger vocabulary and varied sentence structure.

 The YELLOW LEVEL presents more challenging ideas, a broad vocabulary, and wide variety in sentence structure.

 The GREEN LEVEL presents more complex ideas, an extended vocabulary range, and expanded language structures.

 The ORANGE LEVEL presents a wide range of ideas and concepts using challenging vocabulary and complex language structures.

When sharing a content focused book with your child, read to find out facts and concepts, pausing often to restate and talk about the new information. The realistic story format provides an opportunity to talk about the language used, and to learn about reading to problem-solve for information. Encourage children to measure, make maps, and consider other situations that allow them to apply what they are learning.

There is no right or wrong way to share books with children. Find time to read and share new learning with your child, and pass on the legacy of literacy.

Adria F. Klein, Ph.D.
Professor Emeritus
California State University
San Bernardino, California

Editor: Jill Kalz
Designers: Abbey Fitzgerald and Tracy Davies
Page Production: Ashlee Schultz
Art Director: Nathan Gassman
Associate Managing Editor: Christianne Jones
The illustrations in this book were created with ink and digital painting.

Picture Window Books
5115 Excelsior Boulevard
Suite 232
Minneapolis, MN 55416
877-845-8392
www.picturewindowbooks.com

Printed in the United States of America.

All books published by Picture Window Books
are manufactured with paper containing at least
10 percent post-consumer waste.

Library of Congress Cataloging-in-Publication Data
Blackaby, Susan.
Todd's fire drill / by Susan Blackaby ; illustrated by Justin Greathouse.
p. cm. — (Read-it! readers. Social Studies)
Summary: After learning about fire safety at school, Todd makes a map of his house,
marking two exit routes from each room, and conducts a fire drill for his family.
Includes activities.
ISBN-13: 978-1-4048-2332-7 (library binding)
ISBN-10: 1-4048-2332-8 (library binding)
[1. Fire drills—Fiction. 2. Safety—Fiction. 3. Family life—Fiction. 4. Schools—
Fiction.] I. Greathouse, Justin, 1981– ill. II. Title.
PZ7.B5318Tod 2007
[E]—dc22   2007005356

Todd's
Fire Drill

by Susan Blackaby
illustrated by Justin Greathouse

Special thanks to our advisers for their expertise:

Mark Harrower, Ph.D.
Assistant Professor, Department of Geography
University of Wisconsin, Madison

Adria F. Klein, Ph.D.
Professor Emeritus, California State University
San Bernardino, California

PICTURE WINDOW BOOKS
Minneapolis, Minnesota

One Friday afternoon, Chief Murphy visited the second-grade class at Parson's School. She talked about fire safety. "What should you do when you hear the fire alarm?" she asked the class. "Hide under your desk?"

"No!" the class said.

"Call your mom or dad on your cell phone?" Chief Murphy asked.

"No!" the class said again.

"We're supposed to move quickly to the door," said Todd. "Then we march outside, onto the soccer field."

Chief Murphy nodded. "Very good," she said. "And how do you know where to go?"

"We have a map on the wall," said Kat. She pointed to a drawing of the classroom. "The map shows the ways out. The door is our main exit. But if we can't get out that way, we go out the window."

"We had a fire drill earlier this week, too," said Madison.

"Good," said Chief Murphy. "It's important to practice, practice, practice."

Chief Murphy told the class that it was important to have fire drills at home, too. She drew a floor plan of a house. Looking at the drawing was like looking down on a house without its roof. Chief Murphy marked all of the doors and windows. Then she drew arrows to show the exit routes.

"This weekend, I want you all to practice EDITH," Chief Murphy said.

"Edith who?" asked Kat.

Chief Murphy smiled. "In fire safety, EDITH isn't a 'who.' EDITH is a 'what.' It stands for Exit Drills In The Home," she explained.

"For your homework, I want each of you to draw a floor plan of your house," Miss Webb said. "And I'd like you all to draw to the same scale. One inch on your floor plan should equal 6 feet in your house."

"Show two exit routes out of every room," Chief Murphy added. "Then, pick a place outside where your family can meet in case of a fire."

Just then, the bell rang, and the kids packed up their things.

"Have a good weekend!" Miss Webb said.

"Good luck with your maps—and EDITH!" Chief Murphy said.

When Todd got home from school, he measured all of the rooms in the house. He measured the hallways, too. Then he got out a sheet of paper, a pencil, some colored markers, and a ruler. His little sister, Jill, was by his desk in a flash.

"Do you want to play?" she asked.

"No, I'm busy," Todd said. "I'm getting ready for EDITH."

"Edith?" asked Jill. "Is company coming?"

"No, I'll tell you later," said Todd.

13

Once Todd finished drawing the floor plan of his house, he marked the exit routes from his bedroom. He drew a solid red line to show Route 1. The line went from his bedroom door, left down the hall, to the front door. Then Todd drew a dotted green line to show Route 2.

Next, Todd made a small box called a key in the lower-left corner of the map. The key showed what the map's red lines, green lines, and yellow star meant.

Jill poked her head into Todd's room. "Do you want to play now?" she asked.

"I can't," said Todd. "I have homework. I'm making a map of our house. It will show us how to escape in case of a fire."

16

"When is Edith coming?" Jill asked. "Is she coming before the fire?"

Todd shook his head and smiled. He explained that EDITH stood for Exit Drills In The Home. "During a drill, we practice what to do in case of a real fire," he said.

Todd pointed to the map. "Here is your room, Jill," he said. "If you hear the smoke alarm, crawl out your door and turn right. Go through Mom and Dad's room and out the back door—fast!" Todd marked the route in red.

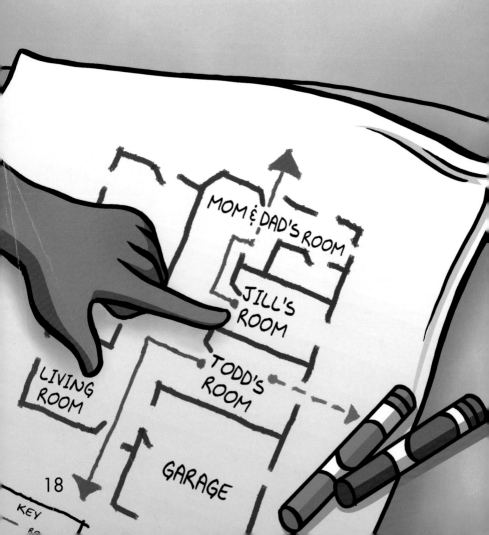

MOM & DAD'S ROOM

JILL'S ROOM

LIVING ROOM

TODD'S ROOM

18

GARAGE

KEY

"But check your door first," Todd continued. "If it feels hot, don't open it. Open the window and hop out." He marked Jill's Route 2 with a green dotted line.

"What about my toys?" asked Jill.

"No toys," Todd said. "Just you!"

Todd drew two exit routes from every room in the house.

"Now can we play?" asked Jill.

"No, we need a meeting place," said Todd.

"How about the garage?" asked Jill.

20

"It needs to be a place that's away from the house," Todd explained. "And it has to be easy to find." He looked out the window and pointed to a big tree in the yard next door. "Like that!" he cried.

Todd marked the meeting place on the map with a yellow star.

Todd showed the finished map to Jill. "OK," he said, "now let's go to your room."

Jill cheered. "What do you want to play first?" she asked.

"We're not going to play yet," Todd said. "We're going to practice EDITH."

Jill frowned. "But I'd rather play," she said.

"I know, but this is important," Todd said. "BEEP-BEEP-BEEP!"

Jill jumped.

"Pretend that's the smoke alarm, Jill," Todd said. "What do you do?"

23

Jill dropped to her hands and knees. She crawled quickly to the door and felt it. "The door isn't hot," she said, "so I go out into the hallway and turn right. Right?"

"Right!" Todd said, crawling behind her. "Keep going through Mom and Dad's room and out the back door."

Mom met the kids in the hallway. "What kind of game is this?" she asked.

"It's not a game, Mom," Todd said, giving her the map. "It's a home fire drill."

"When you hear BEEP-BEEP-BEEP! go fast," said Jill. "No toys. Just you!"

"And once you get outside, meet at the big tree," said Todd.

"I should practice, too," Mom said. "You two go to your rooms, and I'll go to the living room. Todd, when you're ready, start beeping!"

Everyone got set.

BEEP-BEEP-BEEP! BEEP-BEEP-BEEP!
BEEP-BEEP-BEEP!
    The real smoke alarm in the kitchen
was beeping!

Todd dropped down and crawled quickly
to the front door. Mom was right in front of him.
They ran to the tree and met Jill.

"That beeping sounded so real!" Jill said.

"It *was* real!" said Todd.

"Where's Dad?" Jill asked.

Just then, Dad came out the front door. He was holding Todd's map. "Nice job on the fire drill," he said. "Hearing you talk about fire safety reminded me to test our smoke alarm."

"It works, Dad!" Todd said.

Mom smiled. "And so does your map, Todd!" she said.

Activity: Making a Fire Exit Map

What You Need:
- graph paper
- a pencil
- colored pencils or markers
- a ruler

What You Do:
1. Using Todd's floor plan as a guide, draw a floor plan of your house. Include all doors and windows.
2. Mark two ways out of every room. Mark the main exit routes with a solid red line. Mark the second exit routes with a dotted green line.
3. Mark an outside meeting place with a yellow star.
4. Draw a key in the lower-left corner of your map to explain what the star and lines mean.
5. Show your finished map to your family. Plan monthly fire drills so everyone knows what to do in case of a fire.

Glossary

exit—a way out

floor plan—a drawing of a room or rooms as if viewed from above

key—the part of a map that explains what the map's symbols (for example, lines, shapes, and pictures) mean

route—a way, path, or road

scale—the size of a map or model compared to the actual size of things they represent, or stand for

To Learn More

At the Library

Cuyler, Margery. *Stop Drop and Roll.* New York: Simon & Schuster Books for Young Readers, 2001.

Raatma, Lucia. *Fire Safety.* Chanhassen, Minn.: Child's World, 2004.

Sweeney, Joan. *Me on the Map.* New York: Crown, 1996.

On the Web

FactHound offers a safe, fun way to find Web sites related to this book. All of the sites on FactHound have been researched by our staff.

1. Visit *www.facthound.com*
2. Type in this special code: 1404823328
3. Click on the FETCH IT button.

Your trusty FactHound will fetch the best sites for you!

Look for all of the books in the *Read-it!* Readers: Social Studies series:

The Carnival Committee (geography: map skills)
Groceries for Grandpa (geography: map skills)
Lost on Owl Lane (geography: map skills)
Todd's Fire Drill (geography: map skills)